TO DAISY AND DALLY

All quotations contained in this
book are acknowledged at the end

What is sung at the cradle carries itself to the grave

First published 2005 by Sidgwick & Jackson
an imprint of Pan Macmillan Publishers Ltd
Pan Macmillan, 20 New Wharf Road, London N1 9RR
Basingstoke and Oxford
Associated companies throughout the world
www.panmacmillan.com

ISBN 0 283 07031 5

1 3 5 7 9 8 6 4 2

A CIP catalogue record for this book is available from
the British Library.

Designed by Rafaela Romaya
Colour Reproduction by Aylesbury Studios Bromley Ltd
Printed and bound by Bath Press

SAFE FROM HARM

written by Rollo Armstrong
illustrated by Jason White

(the best words in the best order)

Children have little moments of very great power

Jack, aged nearly ten, decided
he was never going to eat again.

Tender are a mother's dreams

But her babe is not what he seems

See him plotting in his mind

To grow up some other kind

For many hours Mr and Mrs tried everything
to make Jack eat his vegetables and fishes.

It's easy to **fly into a passion** – anybody can do that – **but to be** angry **with the right** person,
at **the right time,** to **the right extent and in the right way – well,** that's not easy

Until finally,

I HATE + LOVE:

how can that be?

i don't know

i feel the agony

'Straight to bed,' Mr said.

Justice: n: doing what you like
Injustice: n: being prevented

MYSELF AND ME
SEEM SOMETIMES TO ACT
QUITE DIFFERENTLY.
I SAY, 'DON'T CRY.'
HE SAYS, 'I'LL CRY A LOT.'
I SAY, 'LET'S SLEEP INSTEAD.'
HE SAYS, 'I'D RATHER NOT.'

And there Jack lay, feeling anger, sorrow, bitterness and dismay.

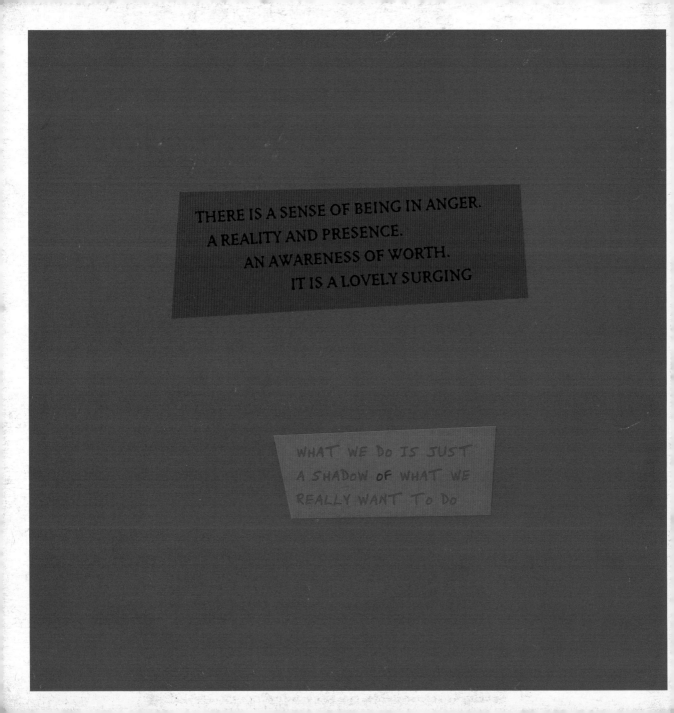

THERE IS A SENSE OF BEING IN ANGER.
A REALITY AND PRESENCE.
AN AWARENESS OF WORTH.
IT IS A LOVELY SURGING

WHAT WE DO IS JUST
A SHADOW OF WHAT WE
REALLY WANT TO DO

'I'm an orphan now!' he exclaimed.
'My ex-parents shall feel the loss and the shame.

I shall run away.'

courage is a kind of salvation

the universe will always bear us company

So from the house that was no longer his home

Jack set out into the dark world alone . . .

As he walked the clouds cleared and
light fell across his path,

for there the moon now hung – so near,

Night, when words fade and things come alive

so bright, so full, so clear.

JUST AROUND the CORNER iS A WORLD OF THINGS that DIdN'T HAPPEN

You don't need eyes to see - you just need vision

Then, before Jack's eyes,
to his great surprise,

If we meet no strangeness, it's because we harbour none

the lamps turned to trees and a forest, dark
and brooding, settled over the street.

The earth moved beneath Jack's feet and Jack
noticed (wow!) where the moon's rays landed

as if all this fever of living were simplicity itself

the strangest animal sat.
Just as Jack regarded it,
it regarded Jack.

'Come follow me,' the monster said.
'Come follow me . . .'

It's easier to stay out of the words than get out

And Jack did, far into the forest, where no birds are
heard, no spiders or cobwebs, no mice with night-eyes,
not a leaf that stirs. The trees that touch the clouds,
the silence that is dense and loud: no wolves, no badgers,
no foxes, no snakes, no water, no breeze – just the
stillness, the closeness, just the moon and just the trees.

There is no limit to how
complicated things can get —
on account of one thing always
leading to another.

everything is easier to recognise
than to define

'Look ahead, young man,' the small monster said
and Jack saw a gentle glow, that as they came nearer
seemed to grow – until the trees parted and Jack saw
in the clearing a small fire had been started.

At the fire lots of big monsters sat
eating fried hamster and having a chat.

The secret thoughts of man run over all things. Holy, profane, clean & Obscene, Monsters & Angels, grave & light: without shame nor blame

WE CAN ONLY BE CERTAIN ABOUT THINGS WE DO NOT FULLY UNDERSTAND

Slurp

& Yum

EVERY LIFE IS MANY DAYS, DAY AFTER DAY.
WE WALK THROUGH OURSELVES, MEETING ROBBERS,
GHOSTS, MONSTERS, GIANTS, OLD MEN, YOUNG MEN,
WIVES, WIDOWS, BROTHERS-IN-LOVE,
BUT ALWAYS MEETING OURSELVES

THOSE MOMENTS — WHAT MOMENTS — WHEN
EVERYTHING IS CLEAR: WHERE TO GO, WHAT TO
DO — IT ALL TAKES CARE OF ITSELF, AND ONE
DOESN'T HAVE TO ASK ABOUT ANYTHING

'We've been waiting for you, young man,' said Old Crooked Face,
the leader of the monsters' gang.

tender handed, stroke a nettle
& it stings for its pains
Grip it like a man of mettle
And soft as silk it remains

To make us feel small in the right way is a function of art

'All monsters to the ready – and you, young sir, climb up.
We have orders to take you to the mountain top.'
'Gosh,' said Jack, 'that is a very,

very,

The heights by great men reached and kept were not attained by sudden flight,

very

long way.'

but they, while their companions slept, were toiling upward in the night

They walked for hours, rising above the forest and up the mountainside, sometimes singing monster songs,* but mostly serious and quiet.

* A Typical Monster Song

At the very top the monsters stopped: 'From here you go alone.'
So Jack slid off Old Crooked Face's scaly back.

He slowly approached the stone, unsure but determined,
where a figure, still and silent, sat.

The infinite possibility of seeing and the impossibility of capturing it

The figure turned and Jack saw it was a boy —
and more than this: the boy's face was the same as his.

When myself & I (and the other?) meet together there can be peace

And the clothes he wore were as Jack's own,
and his manner, his look, his everything –
it was Jack or Jack was him!
In his hand this boy held a golden horn.

I DO NOT KNOW WHAT I HAVE GIVEN YOU

I DO NOT KNOW WHAT YOU HAVE RECEIVED

WHEN I GIVE, I GIVE MYSELF

He reached out and gave it to Jack.

Jack took a deep breath of the cold mountain air,
and blew a glorious, soaring fanfare.

OTHERS BREAK US, BUT WE MEND OURSELVES

Each feels himself most free where his feeling of living is at its greatest

The music filled the night, and as Jack walked the monsters fell in behind;
as if in a trance they rushed and danced down the mountainside.

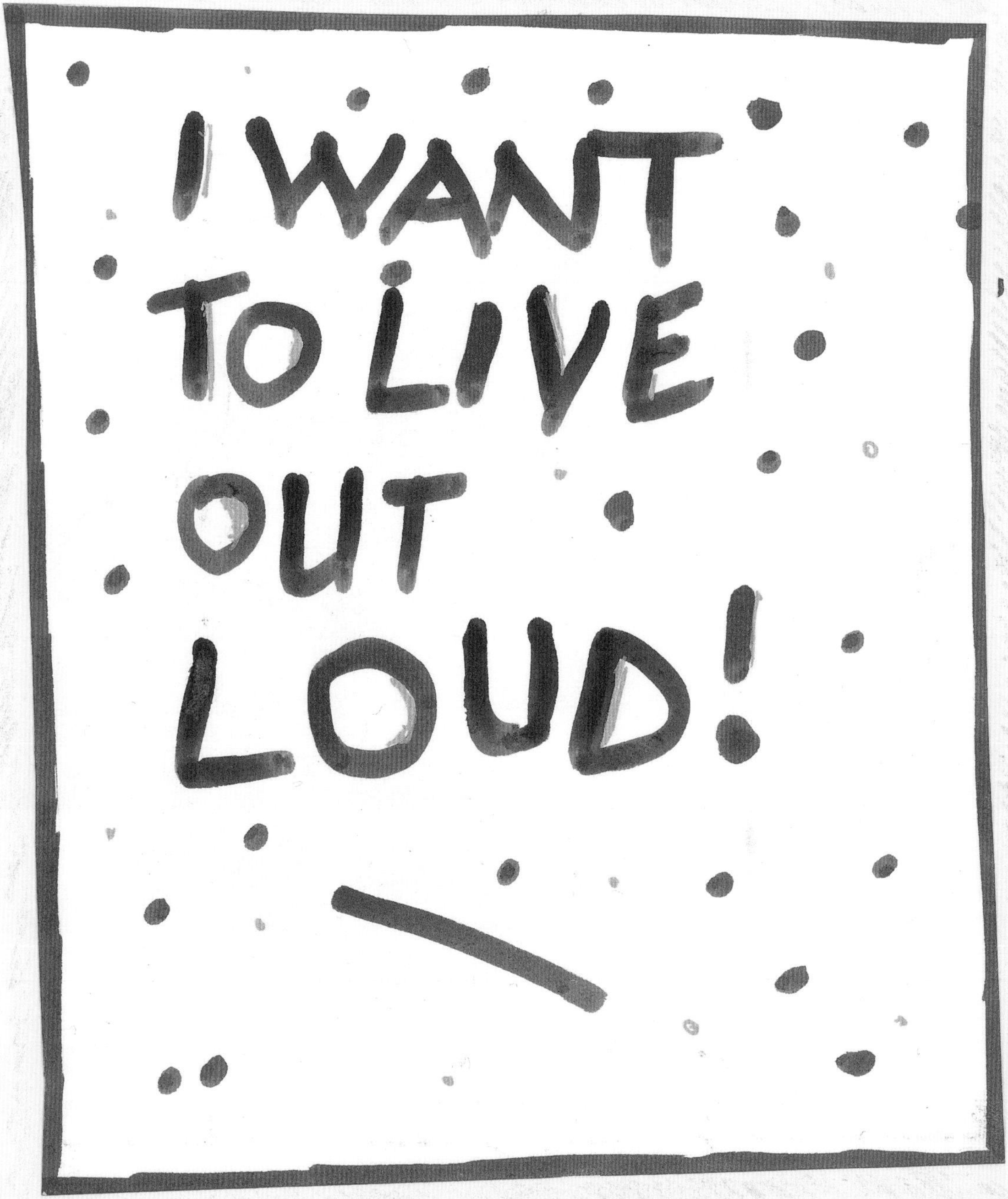
I WANT TO LIVE OUT LOUD!

Back through the forest he led them all.
What had seemed like hours going
– coming back, felt like no time at all.

Out of nowhere Jack's house appeared;
no lights, no pavement, no road –
just the house in the forest, on its own.
So they all came to a stop.

I DID NOT KNOW WHAT I HAD LEFT

UNTIL I RETURNED

Each day contains many **deaths** and **resurrections**

Houses contain us

TRUTH IS A PERMANENT
BLUR IN THE CORNER
OF YOUR EYE

At that moment clouds passed across
the moon, until all the light was gone

and Jack turned to see

Insight: a gust of truth –
in one door, out the other

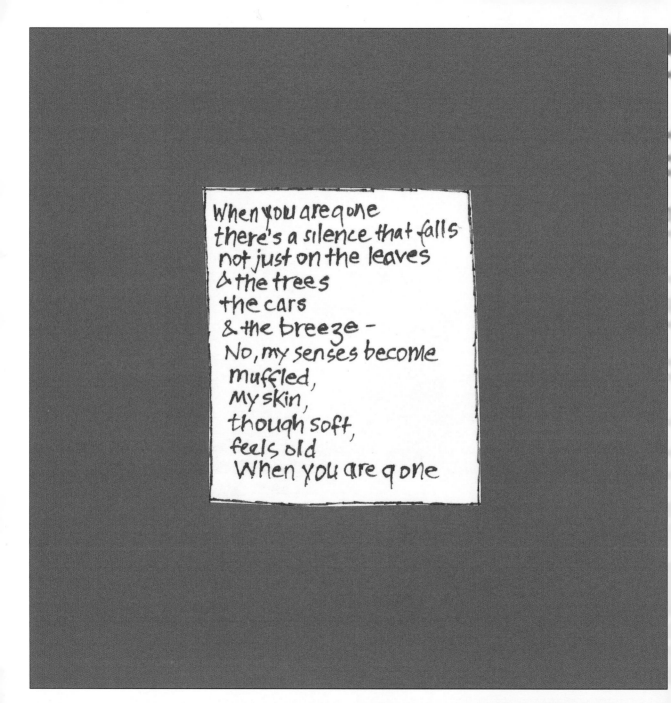

When you are gone
there's a silence that falls
not just on the leaves
& the trees
the cars
& the breeze –
No, my senses become
muffled,
My skin,
though soft,
feels old
When you are gone

the monsters and the forest disappearing silently.

If we do meet again, why we shall smile! If not, why then, this parting was well made

In their place Mr and Mrs stood,
waiting for Jack at their door.

And as Jack turned to face them
it was the strangest thing he saw.

For Mr and Mrs, as – say – night turns to day, were slowly
fading away, and becoming the children they were previously:

The love of a family is like the room you grew up in - the size is known but never measured. It is the love from which all other love flows. It teaches us what love is but it is not a lesson we know we've had until its over and cannot be unlearned.

in fact, the children they will always, always be.

NOTHING EVER ENDS

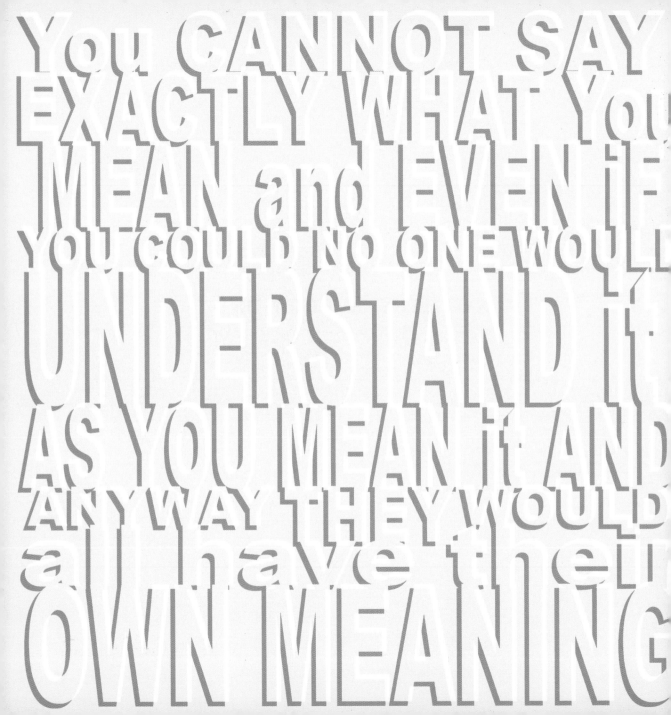

IT JUST BEGINS AGAIN

Isn't It Enough

And as she talked of love that lived on after death
& spirits in the air & karma
& all the ghosts she had seen
And as she talked of Universal connections
& life's ebb and flow
& astronomy and tarot
I thought
'You fool'.

Isn't it enough –
The stars and the moon
The streets and the stones
Art and movies, books and coffee
And the way we build our homes
Isn't it enough –
The love between and within us
The love that is practical & small
Tender & sometimes hardly there
Aren't we enough?

How do planes fly,
Migration, alcohol,
How did we discover olive oil, or wine –
Milk with tea.
Isn't it enough –
Virginia Woolf or T. S. Eliot
Jane Austen or Nabokov
Frasier and the *Sopranos*
The ants at work
Tides and clouds
Space, history, time
Life, every moment of it, every drop of it

IT IS NO SMALL THING
TO HAVE ENJOYED THE SUN,
TO HAVE LIVED LIGHT IN THE SPRING,
TO HAVE LOVED, TO HAVE THOUGHT,
TO HAVE DONE

The stunning album *Safe From Harm*
by Dusted is in all good record shops.

www.dusted-music.com
www.safefromharm.info

ACKNOWLEDGEMENTS: In the order they appear: 'What is sung at the cradle carries to the grave', traditional; 'A child's anger is often bigger than himself', William Armstrong; 'Children have little moments of very great power', Michaela Harris; 'Tender are a mother's dreams', Clarence Day, *Thoughts Without Words*; 'It's easy to fly into a passion', Aristotle, *The Nicomachean Ethics*; 'I hate and love', Catullus; 'One's cruelty is one's power', William Congreve, *The Way of the World*; 'Justice: n: doing what you like', Samuel Butler; 'Myself and me' traditional; 'Perhaps the greatest consolation', Julien Green, *Adrienne Mesurat*; 'There is a sense of being in anger', Toni Morrison, *Beloved*; 'What we do is just a shadow' and 'Against nature's silence I use action', Peter Weiss, *Marat Sade*; 'Go before you think', Daisy Gough; 'Courage is a kind of salvation' Plato, *Republic*; 'The universe will always bear us company', Herman Russe; 'Fear is bigger than God', Dalloway O'Malley; 'The self is more distant than any star', G.K Chesterton, 'The Logic of Elfland'; 'Night, when words fade', Antoine De Saint-Exupéry, *Flight to Arras*; 'Just around the corner', Cornelius Davenport; 'You don't need eyes to see', Maxi Jazz; 'If we meet no strangeness', Robin Laybourne; 'As if all this fever of living', Virgina Woolf, *Mrs Dalloway*; 'Art does not reproduce the visible', Paul Klee, *The Inward Vision*; 'It's easier to stay out of the woods', Dalloway O'Malley; 'Down the street I didn't take', James Lovejoy (in the style of T. S. Eliot); 'There is no limit to how complicated things can get', E.B. White, *Quo Vadimus or the Case for the Bicycle*; 'Everything is easier to recognize than to define', Bernadette Rossetti; 'The secret thoughts of man run over all things', adapted from Thomas Hobbes, *Leviathan*; 'We can only be certain about things', Eric Hoffer, *The True Believer*; 'Every life is many days', James Joyce, *Ulysses*; 'These moments –what moments', Maxim Gorky; 'The calm confidence of a Christian', Mark Twain, *The Adventures of Huckleberry Finn*; 'Tender handed stroke a nettle', traditional; 'To make us feel small in the right way', E. M. Forster, *Two Cheers for Democracy*; 'The heights by great men reached and kept', H.W. Longfellow, 'The Ladder of Saint Augustine'; 'Who are those who walk – always – beside you?', Robin Laybourne; 'Avoiding danger is no safer', Helen Keller; 'A man has reasons', anon; 'Wonder is the foundation of enquiry', Cahar Galbraith; 'The infinite possibility of meaning', Peagram Harrison; 'It's harder to see your own face', Cahar Galbraith; 'When myself and I', Rene Hass; 'I do not know what I have given you', adapted from Antonio Porchia, *Voces*; 'When I give I give myself', Walt Whitman, 'Song to Myself'; 'Others break us', traditional; 'Each feels himself most free', Friedrich Nietzsche; 'I want to live out loud', Emile Zola, *Mes Haines*; 'Music is my first love', The Tavares, 'Music is My First Love'; 'I did not know what I had left', Abbé de Cissé, *Oaths and Poems*, 1746; 'Each day contains many deaths', Fyodor Dostoevsky; 'Houses contain us', William Armstrong; 'Truth is a permanent blur', adapted from Tom Stoppard, *Rosencrantz and Guildenstern Are Dead*; 'Insight: a gust of truth', Dalloway O'Malley; 'When you are gone', Matthew Turner, 'When You Are Gone'; 'If we do not meet again', William Shakespeare, *Julius Caesar*; 'Love is nature's second sun', George Chapman, 'All Fools'; 'The eyes of my eyes were opened', Shri Banghrakhan; 'Our life is what our thoughts make it', Marcus Aurelius, *Meditations*; 'Many events take place', Rainer Maria Rilke, *Letters to a Young Poet*; 'The love of a family', Howard Melville, 'For All I Loved'; 'You cannot say exactly what you mean', F.P. Furlong; 'It is no small thing', adapted from Matthew Arnold, 'Empedocles on Etna'; 'To know, to get to the truth of anything', Thomas Carlyle, *On Heroes*; 'I don't want cheese any more', proverb; 'You will be very unhappy', Harvey Snow; 'Beauty can be unbearable', unknown; 'Truth keeps well until disturbed', Dickon G. Gough, *How I Became Rich*; 'A good answer', Clare Armstrong; 'The real secret of patience is having something to do in the meantime', Barbar Bennett; 'Do I contradict myself?', Walt Whitman, 'Song of Myself'.

To know, to get to the truth
of anything, is a mystic act of
which at best logic can only
bubble on the surface

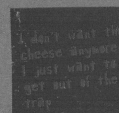

I don't want the
cheese anymore
I just want to
get out of the
trap

YOU WILL BE VERY
UNHAPPY IF YOU EVER
LOVE SOMEONE MORE
THAN YOURSELF

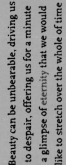

Beauty can be unbearable, driving us
to despair, offering us for a minute
a glimpse of eternity that we would
like to stretch over the whole of time

TRUTH KEEPS WELL UNTIL DISTURBED